KLOOZ

The Secret of the Flying Cows

by J. Banscherus

translated by Daniel C. Baron

illustrated by Ralf Butschkow

Librarian Reviewer
Marci Peschke
Librarian, Dallas Independent School District
MA Education Reading Specialist, Stephen F. Austin State University
Learning Resources Endorsement, Texas Women's University

Reading Consultant
Sherry Klehr
Elementary/Middle School Educator,
Edina Public Schools, MN
MA in Education, University of Minnesota

STONE ARCH BOOKS
Minneapolis   San Diego

First published in the United States in 2008
by Stone Arch Books
151 Good Counsel Drive, P.O. Box 669
Mankato, Minnesota 56002
www.stonearchbooks.com

First published by Arena Books
Rottendorfer str. 16, D-97074
Würzburg, Germany

Copyright © 2004 Jürgen Banscherus
Illustrations copyright © 2004 Ralf Butschkow

Library of Congress Cataloging-in-Publication Data
Banscherus, Jürgen.
   [Das Geheimnis der fliegeden Kühe. English.]
   The Secret of the Flying Cows / by J. Banscherus; translated by
Daniel C. Baron; illustrated by Ralf Butschkow.
   p. cm. — (Klooz)
   "Pathway Books."
   Originally published under title: Das Geheimnis der fliegeden Kühe.
   Summary: While on a much needed vacation at Larry's farm, Klooz
is attacked by flying cows.
   ISBN-13: 978-1-59889-877-4 (library binding)
   ISBN-10: 1-59889-877-9 (library binding)
   ISBN-13: 978-1-59889-913-9 (paperback)
   ISBN-10: 1-59889-913-9 (paperback)
   [1. Vacations—Fiction. 2. Cows—Fiction. 3. Farms—Fiction.
4. Mystery and detective stories.] I. Baron, Daniel C. II. Butschkow,
Ralf, ill. III. Title.
PZ7.B22927Se 2008
[Fic]—dc22   2007006625

Art Director: Heather Kindseth
Graphic Designer: Kay Fraser

1 2 3 4 5 6 12 11 10 09 08 07

Printed in the United States of America

TOP SECRET

Table of contents

KLOOZ
The Secret of the
Flying Cows

CHAPTER 1

Klooz Needs a Vacation

This morning I took my computer in to be fixed. All it has done for the past few days is cough and make funny screaming noises. Frank, one of my classmates, tried to fix it for me. But the noises just got worse.

"A clear case of computer flu," said the man in the computer repair store. He grinned. I was in no laughing mood.

"How much does it cost?" I asked.

The man didn't have to think very long. "One hundred dollars," he said. "And that is a good deal," he added when my mouth fell to my knees.

One hundred dollars. Was he nuts? "Fifty," I said.

"One-hundred," the man said.

"Seventy-five," I suggested.

"Ninety, but just for you, Klooz."

"Eighty."

The man thought for a minute. Then he nodded.

"All right, you win," he said. "Pick it up in two days."

Where am I going to get eighty dollars by the day after tomorrow?

If worst came to worst, I could ask my mom for my allowance for the next nine months.

Not long ago, I was in need of repairs, just like my computer. The first leaves had fallen and my mood was like my last English test — pretty horrible.

When I went to Olga's newspaper stand one afternoon to buy a pack of Carpenter's chewing gum, they were all sold out.

"Not that too!" I moaned.

Olga slid a glass of soda across the counter. "What's wrong, Klooz?" she asked. "Is it a girl?"

Olga had been interested in my love life lately. There was nothing to tell her. Absolutely nothing. Girls are too much stress for me.

"Problems at school?" she asked.

"School," I said. I rolled my eyes.

Olga looked at me with a frown. Then she patted my head.

"You've got to get out, Klooz. Take a week to relax without thieves and crooks. That's what you need," Olga said.

"Vacation?" I laughed. "We don't have enough money for that, Olga. My mom would say no."

"Don't worry, Klooz. I have an idea."

Olga walked to her car.

It was always so shiny that you could see yourself in it.

She took out her cell phone and dialed a number. One week later, I was taking a train to Green Valley to visit her brother.

Green Valley

◄ village ▼ train station fields ►

Missing cow.
Please return
to Farmer
Paulson

When I got off the train, I could see there wasn't much around.

Next to the tracks there were black and white cows. Beyond a small forest, I could see a church and a few houses.

trash

As the train disappeared behind a giant pile of manure, a man approached me. He was as wide as he was tall, and he was wearing a dirty round hat on his big head.

"Klooz?" he asked.

I nodded and reached out my hand to shake his. He squeezed it so hard that I nearly passed out.

"I'm Larry," he said. "Olga's brother."

Without another word, he took the heavy backpack from my shoulder and carried it to a tractor.

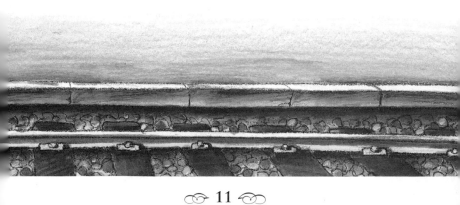

I followed him and climbed into one of the seats. It was just above one of the giant tractor wheels. Larry started the tractor and drove us past the cows and into the woods.

So this was Olga's brother. It was amazing how different they were from each other.

After the phone call with her brother, my friend (and gum seller) had told me that Larry was more than willing to take me for a few days during my fall vacation.

"He's looking forward to meeting you," Olga had said.

If that was true, Larry had an odd way of showing it.

After we had driven through the woods, Green Valley lay before us. The town was just thirty houses crowded around a church. How was I supposed to spend a week here? In the middle of cows, wagons, and old farmers, with the smell of manure in my nose?

My mother didn't want to let me go by myself at first, but Olga talked to her.

Maybe I should have listened to Mom, I thought.

The tractor turned down a dirt road. As we reached the first house, it happened. Something flew through the air and landed in front of us on the road.

Larry braked and came to a stop.

I slammed into his wide back. For a split second I felt like I had just smashed into a tree trunk.

"Everything okay?" he asked after I sat up again. Before I could answer, I saw what had just landed on the road in front of us.

It was a cow.

A big, blue, rubber cow!

"That's impossible!" I wanted to yell.

But I was so amazed by the sight that all I could say was "Tha . . . tha . . ."

"Yup," was all Larry had to say about it. He carefully steered the tractor around the cow.

We went down one short road before driving though a small farm gate.

Larry had just turned the motor off when a girl ran up to us.

"My name is Julie," she said.

Unlike her dad, she didn't crush my hand when she shook it.

"You'll like Larry's daughter," Olga had said when I was buying a bunch of Carpenter's gum from her for the trip.

While Larry disappeared into a barn
next to the house, Julie brought me to
my room on the second floor. On our
way there I told her about the flying
rubber cow.

"Do you have any idea what that
means?" I wanted to know.

She shook her head.
"I have no idea, Klooz.
People around here
are kind of funny
sometimes."

CHAPTER 2

A City Boy in the Country

Early the next morning, I was awakened by the sound of a rooster crowing. It sounded as if the bird was being cooked alive!

The glowing numbers on my watch told me it was a few minutes after five. If the rooster kept crowing like that I might have to make sure it did get cooked.

Luckily for the bird, he stopped crowing a few minutes later and I fell asleep again.

Hours later, I woke up when someone pounded on my door.

"What's going on?" I croaked.

Julie stuck her head in the room. "Hey, sleepyhead," she said, grinning. "Your mom is on the phone."

Mom complained that I hadn't called her the night before. I had promised to do that, but I had forgotten.

"I'm sorry, Mom," I said.

"Everything else okay?" my mom asked.

"Yes," I replied.

If I talked any more, she would have called me three times a day. I certainly didn't need that.

After the phone call I sat down at the kitchen table and ate breakfast. Julie sat down on a stool and watched me. Her mother was away. Otherwise, two women would have been watching me eat.

"Is it exciting?" I asked her.

"Exciting? Is what exciting?" she replied.

"Watching me eat," I said.

"Yup," she said. Then she asked, "Have you ever driven a tractor?"

I almost choked. "T . . . t . . . tractor?" I stuttered.

"Should I teach you how?" she asked.

"Show me how?" I said, gasping.

Julie laughed. "For a city boy, you sure are . . ." She paused.

"I sure am what?" I demanded.

Instead of answering she asked, "Well, what do you do?"

"Well," I began, "I am a private detective."

"I know," she said. "You're the famous Klooz. Aunt Olga told us all about that. What else can you do?"

I began to tell her about the cases I had solved. From the chewing gum mystery to the case of the missing roller skates. From Odin, the biggest dog in the world, to the Circus Zampano.

Before I could really get going she interrupted me.

"Yeah, but what else can you do?"

"Listen," I said. I was starting to get mad. "I am one of the best private detectives in the city."

She interrupted me again. "Can you milk a cow?" she asked.

I shook my head.

"Can you herd animals?"

"No way!" I yelled.

"Can you use an ax?"

I shook my head again.

She pushed her hair back. "I am going to have to teach you everything," she said. She sighed as she jumped down from her stool.

Suddenly my knees felt weak. "You're going to show me how to milk a cow?" I asked.

"If you want," she answered, grinning.

It was clear to me that Julie thought I was pretty wimpy. From her point of view, she was probably right.

On that very day I learned how to drive a tractor. Julie had learned how as a little girl. She drove like an expert. She was also a good teacher.

Even when I had backed over a little birch tree and scraped the farm gate while driving through it, Julie always stayed calm.

"Some people take a little longer to learn than others," she said.

It was a good thing Larry wasn't home. Julie's father had gone to buy a pig. The noises that his tractor was making wouldn't have made him happy.

A few times while I was driving, I had the feeling I was being watched.

Whenever I looked around, though, all I could see were chickens, cows, and pigs.

Julie was all right, if you asked me. She didn't say much, and simply did whatever she felt like doing. She didn't seem to be afraid of anything. Whether she was jumping from really high beams into a pile of hay in the barn or pushing a rude pig out of the way, nothing bothered her.

That's why I shared my Carpenter's gum with her. Usually I just shared with my clients.

"This gum is great," she said. "What's it called?"

"Carpenter's," I said.

"We don't have that kind in Green Valley," she said.

Then Larry returned. He had bought a new pig. Together, we were able to get the pig into his pen. Julie and I held the gate open while Larry pushed him through it.

"Yep," Larry said after we closed the gate. Compared to her dad, Julie was a chatterbox.

I was tired because of all the fresh country air and all the new things I had learned. I walked to my room to take a nap. In my bed, I discovered something that nearly knocked my socks off.

It was a cow's tail! A hairy cow tail and two old bleached bones! At first I wanted to scream and run out of the room. Then I remembered that Julie already thought I was pretty wimpy. So I put the tail and bones in the closet.

I climbed into bed and put a piece of gum in my mouth. The tail and bones hadn't flown into my room, so somebody must have been in here.

Who could it have been? Julie was with me all day. Larry had been out buying the pig. Who was this mystery person? What were they trying to tell me? Even though I was tired, it still took me a while to fall asleep.

I had come to Green Valley to get some rest, but I couldn't resist a case. At least then I wouldn't get rusty.

CHAPTER 3

The First Suspect

That night I slept like a log.

Either somebody had strangled that rooster, or I was so tired that I didn't hear it crowing.

I found Julie the next morning with the pigs.

The pigs were eating their breakfast.

Julie was washing her hands in a sink on the wall.

"Good morning, Klooz," she said.

"Come with me," I said. "I need to show you something."

I had put the cow tail and bones on the bed the same way I had found them the night before.

"Well?" I asked.

"Well what?" Julie replied.

"Do you have any idea who would have done something like that?" I asked.

Julie thought hard about it and then said, "Yep."

"Yep what?" I asked.

"Henry," she said. "It was definitely Henry."

"Who's Henry?"

"He's a boy in my class at school," Julie said. "He lives in town. His dad is a mechanic. It might be that he wants to scare you off."

"Scare me off? Why?" I asked.

Julie's face turned red. "Well," she mumbled.

"He likes you," I said.

"Could be," she said.

"So now you think he might be jealous," I said.

She nodded.

"How did he get in here?" I asked.

"We're in the country, Klooz! Nobody locks their doors," Julie said, laughing.

A few minutes later we were standing in a garage where Henry's dad worked.

Henry's dad told us that Henry wasn't there. He was playing soccer with some friends. Julie knew where he would be.

We found a group of boys playing on a field behind the church. They were playing two on two and the goal was just an old crate. It had rained a lot in the last week. The field was so muddy that it looked like the boys had just climbed out of a pile of manure.

"Henry!" Julie called to him.

The biggest of the four boys turned and walked toward us. He was at least a head taller than I was. If he wanted to beat me up, I wouldn't have had a chance against him. Of course, I hoped it wouldn't come to that. I hate violence.

"This is Klooz," Julie said.

I stuck my hand out to shake his, but he ignored it.

"Hello," I said. I continued, "Look, just leave me alone during my vacation here. It's better for both of us. Okay?"

Henry shifted his weight from one foot to the other and said nothing. Either he didn't understand plain English or he was quieter than Julie's father.

"You're not going to chase me away with cow tails and bones," I said. I took a step toward him.

I didn't want Henry to think that I was scared of him.

Finally he opened his mouth. A noise came out that sounded something like "Huh?"

"Didn't you put those things on my bed?" I asked.

Henry rolled his eyes at me. Then he turned to Julie and said, "For a famous detective, this guy sure isn't very smart, is he?"

When Julie didn't reply, he shrugged his shoulders and went back to his friends. They had been watching us from the field.

Julie and I walked silently back to her father's farm. I didn't have any idea what was going through her head.

I was really mad. Partly at Henry, but mostly at myself. I had behaved like an amateur. I thought a farm boy would be no match for me. And then I had embarrassed myself in front of Julie.

What's the first rule in the detective's handbook? Leave your suspect alone until you have proof! Now Henry knew I suspected him.

"Hey, Klooz," Julie said finally. "Henry is actually a good guy. Even in kindergarten he thought he had to protect me. He'll leave you alone now."

The evening was pretty quiet. When I was about to go to bed, Larry turned to me and asked, "Well?"

"I beg your pardon?" I asked. Mom taught me that. She said it was polite.

"Do you like it here?" he asked.

"Yep," I replied.

Before I went to bed I searched my room. The tail and bones were gone. That didn't surprise me at all. Henry wasn't the first person to get rid of evidence that made him look guilty. The guy was smarter than I had thought.

CHAPTER 4

Another Flying Cow?

The next day, Julie and I drove with Larry into his fields. Parts of his fence had fallen over and we had to set them up again.

I asked him if he thought someone had tipped them over as a joke. He just shrugged his shoulders.

In the field next to the train station there were about twenty posts that had fallen over.

Larry got off of the tractor with a heavy wooden hammer in his hands. He showed me how to hold the posts. Then he hit them so hard with the hammer that it seemed like he wanted them to disappear into the ground forever.

On the way back, Larry stopped the tractor at the only store in Green Valley. The faded sign over the door read "Everything At Vera's." I decided to ask if they had any computer magazines. I wasn't too hopeful.

As I walked to the doorway I looked up. Just then I saw something flying through the air toward me.

At the last second I dove to the ground and rolled, just as an enormous cow hit the street.

The cow landed exactly where I had
been standing just a second before.

Julie jumped from the tractor. Her face was as white as a sheet. "Are you all right?" she asked in a panic.

I stood up. "Everything is okay," I replied.

That wasn't exactly true. My right elbow hurt really bad, but I didn't want to look wimpy in front of Julie again.

I pointed at the cow. "That thing could have killed me," I mumbled.

Julie kneeled by the animal. She hit it on the head and back, laughing the whole time. "Look, Klooz," she said. "This isn't a real cow."

I went closer and took a better look. She was right.

The cow was made out of rubber.

Wool had been pulled over its head, and the eyes were made out of two black buttons. The body was wrapped in dark brown cloth.

"Pick it up!" Julie ordered. "Go on, pick it up!"

I hesitated for a second before picking it up. It was light as a feather.

If it had landed on me, the worst it could have done was give me a bruise.

Then Larry came out of the store.

He was carrying new rubber boots.

"Look, Dad!" Julie said.

"Yep," Larry replied.

"That's the cow from last year's school play, remember?" Julie said.

"Yep," Larry replied.

"Somebody threw it at Klooz," Julie told him.

"Yep," Larry replied.

Then Larry got back onto the tractor and drove away. It seemed as if he had forgotten about us. He drove away and left us in front of the store in the pouring rain.

"Sometimes he is a little . . ." Julie started to say.

"Forgetful," I finished.

When we got back to the farm we were completely soaked. While Julie dried her hair, I took a shower. I didn't want to catch a cold during vacation, and I certainly didn't want to catch a cold in Green Valley.

A while later we met in the living room. Julie had made us some hot cocoa. With the hot cup in one hand, Julie flipped through a magazine with the other.

"So, what do you think of all this?" I asked after a while.

She shrugged her shoulders.

"I know it wasn't Henry," she told me.

I took a big gulp of the cocoa. It was delicious.

"How can you be so sure?" I asked.

"He went on vacation this morning," Julie said. "He and his parents went to Mexico."

"To Mexico?" I asked. That threw all of my ideas out the window. "Well, who was it then? Do you have any idea?"

"Maybe it wasn't on purpose," she said. "Maybe the cow just happened to fall out of a window."

"Just happened to fall?" I laughed. "When I first arrived in Green Valley, your dad picked me up and a cow came flying at the tractor. Then I found a cow tail and two bones in my bed. And today somebody tried to crush me with a giant rubber cow. That can't be a coincidence."

"Yeah, you're probably right," she admitted.

"Somebody in this town wants to chase me away. There isn't any other explanation," I told her.

Julie frowned. "But why would someone want that? What have you done to them, Klooz?"

"I haven't done anything," I said.

I sat in the living room thinking about the case. Then it hit me. The only person it could have been was Larry.

"Who lives above that store?" I asked.

"My Aunt Vera," Julie answered. "She's Aunt Olga's sister."

"And your dad's sister," I said.

Now everything made sense. Larry had someone throw the rubber cow at us when I first arrived.

He put the cow tail and bones in my bed. And the rubber cow? He pushed it out of his sister's apartment. But what did Larry have against me?

Did he think that my vacation in Green Valley was part of some kind of secret plan?

Did he think that Olga had actually hired me to investigate him?

Did he have something to hide that Olga wasn't supposed to know about? I would find out. I wasn't much of a tractor driver, but I was a great detective.

CHAPTER 5

A Secret Door

When I woke up the next morning it was still dark outside. Rain pounded on the attic window above my bed.

As a detective, I have to spend a lot of time outdoors.

I still don't like wet clothes and soaked shoes.

On the other hand, I was pretty sure that I wouldn't have to go outside today.

The solution to the riddle, if I was correct, was hidden somewhere close by.

I tried to fall asleep again, but I couldn't.

I walked from my room to the kitchen, but I didn't hear a sound.

Julie and Larry seemed to be gone. That was okay with me.

That way I would have time to take a look around.

After breakfast, I put a piece of gum in my mouth and got started.

I went through the house from top to bottom.

I looked in closets and boxes, and under beds and loose floorboards.

I found dusty deer antlers, old newspapers, a cowboy hat, and old jewelry, but nothing that was very helpful to my case.

Finally I left the house and walked through the pouring rain to a nearby barn.

The door to the barn was open. Inside, I could see a light on behind a plow and a tractor trailer.

I carefully crept between the plow and trailer to get a better look. I was trying as hard as I could to not be seen.

The light was coming from a square hole in the floor of one of the stalls.

A door in the floor, which usually hid the hole, was open. I didn't remember seeing it before.

Two days ago Julie and I had been in this barn together. The trailer had been parked right over the secret door in the floor.

My heart began to beat faster. That always happens right before I solve a case.

I quietly left my hiding place and crept closer to the opening. A ladder in the hole led to a kind of basement underneath it. All I could see was a cement floor.

I wondered if Larry had someone held prisoner down there. What if Julie's dad was a kidnapper and he wanted to get rid of me with flying cows so I wouldn't find out about him?

For just a second, I thought I should call the police. Then again, Green Valley was too small to have a police officer and it would take a while before one arrived from a larger city. That might be too long for the person who Larry had kidnapped.

I pulled my courage together and started down the ladder. It shook as I climbed down. About halfway down the ladder, one of the rungs broke with a loud crack. I pressed myself against the ladder. I was afraid to even take a breath.

I waited for a few seconds. It seemed no one had heard anything.

Finally, I reached the floor. I turned toward the light, and was completely surprised by what I saw.

Julie and Larry were in one corner of the huge underground room.

But there wasn't a kidnapped person, like I thought I would see.

No, instead there was a motorcycle.

A really old motorcycle.

Larry was oiling its drive chain while Julie wiped the exhaust pipe with a towel.

"Hello!" I said as I walked over.

Larry turned around and stared.

Julie smiled at me and kept working.

"Nice motorcycle," I said.

"Yep," Larry replied.

"Definitely an old one," I said.

"Yep," Larry replied.

"And valuable," I said.

Larry stood up and said, "Well, you've caught me now, Klooz."

"I beg your pardon?" I asked, surprised.

Larry wiped his oily fingers on his pants.

He looked at Julie and said, "Would you go to Aunt Vera's and pick up some tomatoes for lunch?"

It was clear that Larry wanted to talk to me alone.

Julie left. Larry and I were alone. He walked over to the motorcycle and petted the gas tank. "This is an old Triumph," he said. "There are only ten like it in the whole world."

When I didn't say anything, he continued, "Olga always has been a smart lady. She asked if you could come to the farm, and she knew I couldn't say no. Refusing to let you come here would have made me look guilty."

So that's what it was all about. "The motorcycle belongs to Olga," I said.

"Yep. Our father died three years ago and he left this motorcycle to Olga," Larry said.

"And you told her that it was stolen, right?" I guessed.

"Yep."

"Why?" I asked.

He patted the handlebars. "I was the one who always took care of this motorcycle, even when I was a little boy. And then my father went and left it to Olga just because she likes old vehicles."

"You wanted to chase me away with cow attacks," I said.

He nodded.

"And now?" I asked.

Larry sighed. "Tell Olga she can pick up the Triumph. So, do you still want to stay here until your vacation ends?"

"Yep," I said.

As we were climbing the ladder I wanted to know just one more thing, "Who threw the blue cow in front of the tractor we were riding in?"

"I have no idea," he said. "Really. It was probably just some kid, but I saw how shocked you were and it gave me the idea."

"You thought that you could get rid of me with a cow tail, bones, and a rubber cow," I said. He nodded.

"And what about Julie?" I asked.

Larry stared down at the floor. "She doesn't know anything about all of this."

"Just so you know, Olga just wanted me to come here to relax," I told him.

The rest of my time in Green Valley was great. Not only did I become a really good tractor driver, I also milked my first cow. A real cow. Without any help at all!

Whenever I could, I helped Julie and Larry in the fields and in the barn.

Larry still never said much, and I couldn't hold that against him anyway.

When they finally brought me to the train station on Saturday afternoon, Larry growled, "Tell Olga I say hello."

"From me too," Julie added.

"You should come visit me next year," I said to her.

She nodded. "I promise."

A day later I went to Olga's newsstand and told her about the flying cows and my discovery under the barn.

I ended my report by saying, "Larry said you could pick up the motorcycle whenever you wanted."

She gave me a soft drink. Then she said, "I don't want it."

"You don't want it?" I asked, surprised.

"It was always Larry's motorcycle," Olga answered. "He should keep it. You know, Klooz, I never did believe that it had been stolen."

Suddenly, it was like a light bulb went off in my head.

"You sent me to Larry's farm so I would find that motorcycle and you would finally know the truth!" I exclaimed.

Olga turned red. "Well, maybe a little," she said quietly.

I slammed my fist on the counter so hard that the glass of soda jumped into the air.

"Your brother was right!" I cried. "You are smart! That's going to cost you twice the normal fee!"

"Ten packs of gum? But, Klooz," Olga said.

"Or else I'll have to get my gum somewhere else," I said.

Olga pushed the packs across the counter toward me.

"What about Julie? Did you get along with her?" Olga asked.

I nodded. "She's going to visit me next year."

Olga smiled. "See, Klooz? I said you needed to relax and make some new friends."

I drank the rest of the soda and put a piece of Carpenter's gum in my mouth.

"Well, isn't that the other reason you sent me to Green Valley?" I said.

The end

About the Author

Jürgen Banscherus is a worldwide phenomenon. There are almost a million Klooz books in print, and they have been translated into Spanish, Danish, Thai, Chinese, and eleven other languages. He has worked as a newspaper writer, a research scientist, and a teacher. His first book for children was published in 1985. He lives with his family in Germany.

About the Illustrator

Ralf Butschkow was born in Berlin. He works as a freelance graphic designer and illustrator, and has published more than 50 books for children. Critics have praised his work as "thoroughly enjoyable," "creatively original," and "highly recommended."

Glossary

amateur (AM-uh-chur)—not a professional

coincidence (koh-IN-si-duhnss)—a chance happening

conspiracy (kuhn-SPEER-uh-see)—a secret plan

convince (kuhn-VINSS)—to make someone believe something

guilty (GIL-tee)—someone who has committed a crime

investigate (in-VES-tuh-gayt)—to search out, hunt for clues

manure (muh-NOO-ur)—animal waste put on land to improve the quality of the soil and make crops grow better

rung (RUHNG)—one of the bars on a ladder

suspect (SUHSS-pekt)—a person who might be guilty of a crime

tractor (TRAK-tur)—a powerful vehicle with large tires. Tractors are often used to pull farm machinery.

Discussion Questions

1. Why does Olga think that Klooz needs a vacation?

2. Why did Olga's father leave her the motorcycle instead of giving it to Larry?

3. At the end of this book, Olga decides to leave the motorcycle with Larry. Why does she do that?

Writing Prompts

1. If you needed a vacation, where would you choose to go? Write about your idea of the perfect vacation.

2. Imagine that you find a mysterious door in a barn's floor. Where does it lead? What do you find when you open it? Is it funny, scary, or mysterious? Write about it!

3. It can be interesting to think about a story from another character's point of view. Try writing chapter 2 from Julie's point of view. What does she think about? What does she see? How does she feel about Klooz?

Internet Sites

Do you want to know more about subjects related to this book? Or are you interested in learning about other topics? Then check out FactHound, a fun, easy way to find Internet sites.

Our investigative staff has already sniffed out great sites for you!

Here's how to use FactHound:

1. Visit *www.facthound.com*

2. Select your grade level.

3. To learn more about subjects related to this book, type in the book's ISBN number: **1598898752**.

4. Click the **Fetch It** button.

FactHound will fetch the best Internet sites for you!